Ever After High™

Meet Crystal Winter

Adapted by Perdita Finn

Based on the screenplay written by
Nina Bargiel, Sherry Klein, MJ Offen,
Audu Paden, and Keith Wagner

LITTLE, BROWN AND COMPANY
New York   Boston

Crystal wanted to play ice hockey
with her parents.

"I'm up for that!" said the Snow King.

The Snow Queen was going to referee.

The palace pixies helped Crystal
lace up her skates.
Crystal should lace up her own skates!
Would Crystal ever be ready to rule?

Jackie the frost elf wanted to rule
the kingdom.

She had an evil plan to take over.

She shared her plan with her brother,
Northwind.

Jackie used dark-pink dust to curse the Snow King and the Snow Queen. The dark-pink dust made them mean!

"You are acting like a spoiled brat!"
the king shouted at Crystal.
Then he turned the Snow Queen into
an ice sculpture!

Crystal did not understand
why her father was acting this way.
She went to see her friends
at Ever After High.
Maybe they could help her!

Crystal brought winter with her
to Ever After High.
It was the first summer snow day
in the history of the school!

But then her father arrived.
He turned the snowstorm into a blizzard.

Then the king took away Crystal's wand. "No ice powers forever after!" he cried. An icy wind chilled Crystal's heart.

Baba Yaga had advice for
Crystal and her friends.
They could cure the king's curse—
but only if they found four magic roses.

The friends ventured out on a sleigh
to find the roses.
The first stop was Rosabella's family castle.
But the Rose of Spring was not in bloom
because of the cold.

But Faybelle worked some magic!

"Two, four, six, eight.

Roses bloom, we cannot wait!"

The girls hopped back on the sleigh.
Except for Crystal.
"Can someone help me lace up my boots?"
she asked.

Ashlynn and Briar taught Crystal
how to tie her laces!

Jackie came out from her hiding spot.
She taunted Crystal
for not knowing how to tie her shoes.
Then Jackie started an avalanche!

The friends were blocked by a wall of snow.
And Crystal's boots were untied again!

Crystal refused to give up.
She tied her laces and climbed
the snow wall all by herself!

They found the Rose of Summer.
It was hidden inside
Cinderella's enchanted pumpkin.
"Yes!" Crystal cheered.

She found the Rose of Fall
in Sleeping Beauty's spinning wheel.

When Jackie's curse put everyone to sleep,
Crystal was the one to wake them up.
Crystal was determined to save the season!

The wicked winter was becoming wilder
and wilder.

A tornado lifted Crystal's sleigh into the air.

They were headed to the Winter Palace!

Blondie updated everyone
at Ever After High.
"Will Crystal Winter be able
to find the final rose?"
Everyone was counting on Crystal!

Crystal made it to the castle.
But Jackie had already
put the king into a deep sleep
and taken over the throne.
Jackie ordered Northwind
to stop Crystal.

Northwind turned himself
into an ice giant.
Crystal was not afraid.
She was brave!

Crystal went to find Jackie,
but her laces were untied again.

Rosabella and Daring wanted to help.
They tricked Northwind.
They dared him to turn into a mouse…
and he did!

Crystal skated into the throne room.
Jackie told Crystal that
Jackie was in charge now.

The palace pixies brought
Crystal her wand!

Now Crystal could fight back—
but she tripped on her laces!

Jackie laughed.

"Come back when you can tie your own shoes!"

But Crystal had already done it.

She turned her wand into a hockey stick, and sent Jackie into the net!

"Goal!" shouted Blondie.

Crystal and her friends cured
the king and queen
with the four magic roses!

The Snow King was so proud of Crystal.
She had saved the season!
Crystal was ready to rule!

"I couldn't have done it without
my friends," said Crystal.
The king gave his scepter to Crystal.

Blondie reported the news.

"This just in, Ever After High!

Prepare yourself for a change in the weather!"